To the Library of Dreams in El Salvador
Para la Biblioteca de los Sueños en El Salvador
— RCL

Text copyright © 2022 by René Colato Laínez • Illustrations copyright © 2022 by Nomar Perez
All Rights Reserved • HOLIDAY HOUSE is registered in the U.S. Patent and Trademark Office.
Printed and bound in September 2021 at C&C Offset, Shenzhen, China.
www.holidayhouse.com • First Edition • 1 3 5 7 9 10 8 6 4 2

Library of Congress Cataloging-in-Publication Data
Names: Colato Laínez, René, author. | Perez, Nomar, 1975- illustrator. Colato Laínez, René. We play soccer. | Colato Laínez, René. We play soccer. Spanish.
Title: We play soccer : in English and Spanish = Jugamos al fútbol : en inglés y español / by René Colato Laínez ; illustrated by Nomar Perez.
Other titles: Jugamos al fútbol
Description: First edition. | New York : Holiday House, [2022] | Series: My friend, mi amigo
Audience: Ages 3-7. | Audience: Grades K-1. | Parallel text in English and Spanish.
Summary: Two boys, an English speaker and a Spanish speaker, play soccer together.
Identifiers: LCCN 2021013739 | ISBN 9780823445066 (hardcover)
Subjects: CYAC: Soccer—Fiction. | Friendship—Fiction. | Spanish language materials—Bilingual. | LCGFT: Picture books.
Classification: LCC PZ73 .C5872 2021 | DDC [E]—dc23
LC record available at https://lccn.loc.gov/2021013739

MY FRIEND | MI AMIGO

We Play Soccer
Jugamos al Fútbol

BY RENÉ COLATO LAÍNEZ

iLLUSTRATED BY NOMAR PEREZ

In English
and Spanish
....
En inglés
y español

FÚTBOL

HOLIDAY HOUSE
NEW YORK

Juguemos al fútbol.

Tengo mis zapatos de fútbol.

I can juggle the ball.

¡Sí, podemos jugar!

Words: Palabras

Ball/Pelota

Cleats/Zapatos de fútbol

Goal/Gol

Hi/Hola

Let's go/Vamos

Let's play/Juguemos

Ready/Listo

Red/Rojo

Soccer/Fútbol

Team/Equipo

To juggle/Hacer malabares

To pass/Pasar

To wait/Esperar

To win/Ganar

Uniform/Uniforme

We play/Jugamos

Yes/Sí